21st Century Basic Skills Library

KIDS CAN USE LESS

by Cecilia Minden, PhD

Cherry Lake Publishing • Ann Arbor, Michigan

3

Published in the United States of America
by Cherry Lake Publishing
Ann Arbor, Michigan
www.cherrylakepublishing.com

Photo Credits: Cover and page 1, ©Philip Scalia/Alamy; page 4, ©argus/Shutterstock, Inc.; page 6, ©Michael Zysman/Shutterstock, Inc,; page 8, ©Eugene Berman/Shutterstock, Inc.; page 10, ©Losevsky Pavel/Shutterstock, Inc.; page 12, ©iStockphoto.com/snapphoto; page 14, ©Hofmeester/Dreamstime.com; page 16, ©Sean Prior/Shutterstock, Inc.; page 18, ©iofoto/Shutterstock, Inc.; page 20, ©Blend Images/Alamy

Library of Congress Cataloging-in-Publication Data
Minden, Cecilia.
Kids can use less/by Cecilia Minden.
p. cm.—(Kids can go green!)
Includes index.
ISBN-13: 978-1-60279-869-4 (lib. bdg.)
ISBN-10: 1-60279-869-9 (lib. bdg.)
1. Energy conservation—Juvenile literature. 2. Water Conservation—Juvenile literature. 3. Environmental protection—Citizen Participation—Juvenile literature. I. Title. II. Series.
TJ163.35.K59 2009
644—dc22 2009049107

Cherry Lake Publishing would like to acknowledge the work of The Partnership for 21st Century Skills. Please visit *www.21stcenturyskills.org* for more information.

Printed in the United States of America
Corporate Graphics Inc.
July 2010
CLFA07

TABLE OF CONTENTS

Why Should Kids Use Less?

We can all help Earth by **reducing**.

Reducing means to use less or make something smaller.

If we use less, we will have less **solid waste**.

Then there will be less trash in our **landfills**.

Trash in landfills should **decompose** back to dirt. Some **products** take many years to do this.

Less use of those products helps keep Earth **green**.

How Can Kids Use Less?

The best way to use less is to buy less.

Stop and think before you buy. Do I really need this or do I just want it?

Buy only what you need.

Look for products that will last a long time. Fix things that break.

Try to **reuse** old things in new ways. That way, you throw less away.

Where Can Kids Use Less?

You can use less at home. Use fewer things made of paper.

Cloth napkins and towels can be washed. Paper ones will become more trash.

Less use of **plastic** bags helps Earth.

Plastic takes a long time to decompose. Plastic bags will still be in a landfill years from now.

You can reduce waste in your classroom, too.

Use both sides of a sheet of paper. You will use a lot less paper.

One Earth
One Person
One Chance

You can use less everywhere you go.

How can you use less today?

Find Out More

BOOK

Kroll, Steven, and Steve Cox (illustrator). *Stuff!: Reduce, Reuse, Recycle*. Tarrytown, NY: Marshall Cavendish, Inc., 2009.

WEB SITE

EEK!—Our Earth

dnr.wi.gov/org/caer/ce/eek/earth/index.htm

Read more about how to help keep Earth healthy.

Glossary

decompose (DEE-kuhm-poze) to break apart or rot

green (GREEN) good for keeping Earth and all its living things healthy

landfills (LAND-filz) places where garbage is piled up

plastic (PLASS-tik) a material made by humans that is light and strong; plastic can be molded into many different shapes

products (PROD-uhkts) things made to be used by people

reducing (ri-DOOSS-ing) making smaller or using less

reuse (ree-YOOZ) to use something again

solid waste (SOL-id WAYST) trash such as paper, metal, glass, plastic, or other materials

Home and School Connection

Use this list of words from the book to help your child become a better reader. Word games and writing activities can help beginning readers reinforce literacy skills.

a
all
and
at
away
back
bags
be
become
before
best
both
break
buy
by
can
classroom
cloth
decompose
dirt
do
Earth
everywhere
fewer
fix
for
from
go
green
have
help
helps
home
how
I
if
in
is
it
just
keep
kids
landfill
landfills
last
less
long
look
lot
made
make
many
means
more
napkins
need
new
now
of
old
ones
only
or
our
paper
plastic
products
really
reduce
reducing
reuse
sheet
smaller
solid
some
something
should
sides
still
stop
take
takes
that
the
then
there
things
think
this
those
throw
time
to
today
too
towels
trash
try
use
want
washed
waste
way
ways
we
what
where
why
will
years
you
your

Index

About the Author

Cecilia Minden is the former Director of the Language and Literacy Program at the Harvard Graduate School of Education. She currently works as a literacy consultant for school and library publishers and is the author of more than 100 books for children.